Vic   APR 1 0 2009

ATOS Book Level: _____4.9_____
AR Points: _____1.0_____
Quiz #: _72217_ ☑RP☐ LS☐ VP
Lexile: _____

For Zona ~ D. K-S.
To Caitlin and her coven ~ B. G.

Text copyright © 2003 by Dick King-Smith
Illustrations copyright © 2003 by Bob Graham

First U.S. edition 2003

Library of Congress Cataloging-in-Publication Data
King-Smith, Dick.
The nine lives of Aristotle / Dick King-Smith ; illustrated by Bob Graham.
p. cm.
Summary: Aristotle, a little white kitten, goes to live with a witch in an old cottage, w
he finds so many opportunities for risky adventures that he soon has only one life le
ISBN 0-7636-2260-5
[1. Cats—Fiction. 2. Witches—Fiction.] I. Graham, Bob, ill. II. Title.
PZ7.K5893Ni 2003
[Fic]—dc21   2003040942

2 4 6 8 10 9 7 5 3

Printed in China

This book was typeset in M Bembo.
The illustrations were done in watercolor and ink.

Candlewick Press
2067 Massachusetts Avenue
Cambridge, Massachusetts 02140

visit us at www.candlewick.com

The Nine Lives of
Aristotle

DICK KING-SMITH

illustrated by BOB GRAHAM

CANDLEWICK PRESS
CAMBRIDGE, MASSACHUSETTS

When Aristotle was a kitten, he did not know that cats have nine lives. His mother knew, of course. But I'm not going to tell him, she thought. He's already a rascal, much bolder than his brothers and sisters, and if he knows that he has nine lives to play with, he'll take all sorts of risks.

So she didn't say anything to Aristotle except "Goodbye" when he left home and went to live with an old lady.

A strange-looking old lady she was, with a beaky nose and a chin that jutted out, and she wore black clothes, and a tall black hat on top of her stringy gray hair.

Her name was Bella Donna, and it was she who decided to call her new kitten Aristotle.

"Really," she said, "I ought to have a black cat, but it'll be a nice change to have a white one."

But the very first day that Aristotle went to live in Bella Donna's funny old cottage, he decided he would explore it from top to bottom. Or rather from bottom to top, because when he looked all around the downstairs rooms and then the upstairs rooms, he thought he'd like to get up on the roof.

It was a thatched roof, so once Aristotle climbed up the creeper that grew on the walls of the cottage, he could easily walk up the thatch to the single chimney.

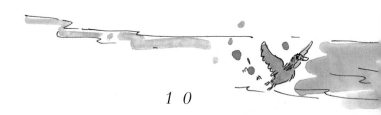

Then, because he was curious, as all cats are, he scrambled up the chimney, looked down, and wondered what the hole was for.

At that very moment, a big puff of smoke came up, right in Aristotle's face, which made him cough and sneeze and lose his balance, and down the chimney he fell.

Bella Donna had just lit her kitchen fire when down into the fireplace came a great load of soot, which put out the flames, and after the soot, a kitten that had been white but was now as black as a witch's hat.

"Well, my boy," said Bella Donna, "that's the first of your nine lives gone. Good thing the chimney was so dirty or you'd have burned to death. You better be a little more careful, Aristotle, if you want to grow to be a cat. Only eight to go."

There was quite a lot of tidying up to do after that. Using a large broomstick that stood in a corner of her kitchen, Bella Donna swept up all the mess that the soot had made. Then she laid the fire again and lit it. She heated some water and, when it was warm enough, she poured it into a big tin basin. Then she picked up Aristotle and put him in the basin and rinsed him and soaped him and rinsed him again.

Aristotle had mixed feelings about all this. On the one hand, like all cats, he hated being dirty, and it was lovely to be a white kitten

again. On the other, he hated water. But once
Bella Donna had rubbed him dry and set a
dish of meat before him, he decided that his
new owner meant him more good than harm.

Aristotle did not know what the meat
was (it was in fact a mixture of frogs' legs,
snails, and fried wood lice), but he thought it
was delicious. He ate it all up, lay down in
front of the fire, and fell fast asleep.

When he woke up again, it was to find himself alone. The old lady had gone, shutting the kitchen door behind her, and so, he noticed, had her broomstick.

Where she had gone he did not know, but what with the big meal he had eaten and the heat of the fire, Aristotle began to feel

very thirsty. He set off to explore the kitchen
for something to drink.

On a table, his eyes told him, stood a large
heavy earthenware jug. He jumped up and
peered into it. It was, his nose told him, full
of milk of some sort, though from which
animal he did not know (it was in fact a

mixture of cow's milk, goat's milk, and ewe's milk, with a dash of pigeon's milk added).

He put a paw down into the jug and stirred the liquid around, which, his ears told him, made an appetizing sloshy sound. He pulled out the paw and licked it, and his tongue told him that it tasted delightful.

Eagerly Aristotle put both paws on the rim of the jug, shoved his head down inside it, and began to drink greedily. As the level of the milk dropped, he pushed more of himself into the heavy jug, until at last it tipped over on top of him.

When, just after midnight, Bella Donna came back, she opened the kitchen door, propped her broomstick in the corner, and then heard a most melancholy mewing.

By the dying light of the fire, she could see that her great earthenware milk jug was standing upside down in the middle of the kitchen table, that there was milk all over both table and floor, and that the noise was coming from inside the upturned jug.

She lit a candle, then lifted the jug to reveal beneath it a whiter than white, wetter than wet, woebegone kitten.

Once more she warmed water to wash
Aristotle. Once more she rubbed him dry.
Once more she addressed him.

"Well, my boy," said Bella Donna,
"that's the second of your lives gone. Good

thing the jug tipped over or you'd have gotten stuck in it, head down, and drowned. You better be a little more careful, Aristotle, or you'll never make old bones. Only seven lives to go."

Dry and warm now, the white kitten looked up at the black-clothed old woman and felt strangely comforted by the sound of her voice.

Before she went to bed, Bella put Aristotle outside.

"I expect you drank a lot of that milk,"

she said to him, "and there's been enough mess in the kitchen without you adding to it." What a rascal he is, she said to herself. He came here only yesterday, but already he's used up two lives. At this rate, he'll never grow into a proper witch's cat.

But in fact Aristotle managed to keep out of trouble for quite a while. A whole week went by, and the white kitten behaved sensibly. He ate his meat and drank his milk and didn't scratch at the curtains or the chair covers and didn't make any messes in the cottage.

Indeed, by the end
of that week, Bella
Donna had trained
him to use a litter box.

"You didn't make a very good start,
Aristotle," she said to him, "but now
you're doing fine. Just keep on keeping
out of mischief." And she crossed her
long knobby fingers.

If Aristotle had gone to an ordinary
home, things might have been different, but
Bella's old cottage was in many ways a risky
sort of place for an adventurous kitten.

It stood in the middle of a little wood in which were many tall trees, and through which flowed a swift steep-banked stream. On one side of the wood there was a twisty road, and on the other a lofty embankment along the top of which ran a railway line. There was also a farm nearby, on which lived a large dog.

Aristotle's next adventure took place up a tall tree. Climbing was something he found he rather liked, and now he often scrambled up the creeper on the cottage walls and up the thatched roof to sit upon the ridgepole at the top (though he kept away from the chimney). He enjoyed this lofty perch, but the cottage was quite a low building and the trees around it were, he could see, much higher.

So one fine morning, Aristotle chose a tall tree and leapt up its trunk onto the lowest branch, and then onto a higher one, and so on up and up, thinking himself such a clever cat.

But the farther up he went, the thinner and more springy the branches became, till at last he found himself

right at the top, clinging
to a thin bough that danced in
the breeze, and he suddenly felt ever
such a scared kitten. The ground, he
could see, was an awful long way down, and
he wind seemed to be getting stronger and
he bough bouncier. He lost his nerve, and his
grip, gave a loud yowl of fright, and fell.

By good
fortune, Bella Donna was
looking out of her open
kitchen window and heard
her kitten's cries and saw
him fall, paws spread wide
tail whirling madly around
and around, down, down,
down, bumping off the
branches as he went.

Let's hope he lands
in the stream, she
thought, and she grabbed

her broomstick and
hurried out.

Luck was on Aristotle's
side, for he did indeed
land, with a great splash, in
water that was very cold
and running very fast. He
swallowed a lot of it as he
struggled and spluttered
and tried in vain to
scramble up the stream's
steep bank. But as he was
swept along, he suddenly

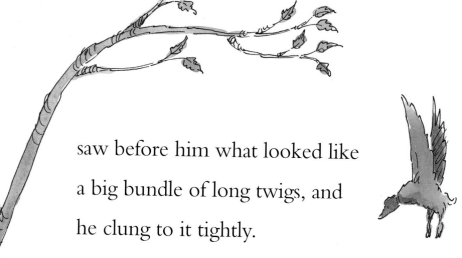

saw before him what looked like
a big bundle of long twigs, and
he clung to it tightly.

Bella Donna raised her broomstick and
lifted her wet white kitten out.

Aristotle was so out of breath that he
could only manage a feeble mew. He clung

as tightly to Bella Donna as he had to her broomstick, while she cuddled him close to make him feel safe again.

"Well, my boy," she said to him after she'd carried him home and rubbed him down, "you've managed to get through two lives in one go. The fall should have broken your little neck, and the stream should have filled your little lungs. It looks as though it'll need a bit of magic to keep you in the land of the living. You really must take more care, Aristotle. Only five lives left now."

Now time passed, quite a lot of time, without Aristotle getting into hot water, or cold water for that matter, or falling out of trees or down chimneys or into milk jugs, as he grew from kitten to cat.

Someone less wise than Bella Donna might have thought that he was over the worst of his troubles, but though Bella might have been old and skinny and ugly, she was also very wise indeed. She knew, in her wisdom, that her white cat would surely have other lives to lose, and so she kept a close eye on him.

Aristotle had grown used to the fact that Bella was around the place mostly by day and that she usually went out at night, leaving him snoozing by the kitchen fire. Being a sharp-eyed animal, he also noticed that she never went out into the darkness without her broomstick, though he did not know why.

By day, Bella Donna was a busy person, so try as she would, there were times when the eye she kept on Aristotle was not as close as it should have been.

For example, she often seemed to be heating something—Aristotle did not know what—in a large black cauldron that hung suspended over the kitchen fire. Whatever was in this cauldron needed a lot of stirring, and one day, while Bella was busy at this, Aristotle slipped out for a walk.

Curious, as all cats are, he had been wondering for some time about a lot of loud noises that came now and again from one side of the wood. There were clanking noises and

puffing noises and sometimes a shrill whistle,
and they got louder and louder as whatever-
it-was drew nearer, and then quieter and
quieter as whatever-it-was went away.

On this particular day, what with the
crackling of the fire and the bubbling of the

liquid in the cauldron, Bella did not hear the clanking and the puffing, but the whistle, when it came, was very loud and very shrill. She looked quickly around the kitchen for Aristotle, but there was no sign of him.

Had anyone been watching, they would have been amazed at how swiftly Bella now acted. First she dropped her ladle into the cauldron. Then she lifted the cauldron off the fire. Then she picked up her broomstick from the corner and dashed out.

It had taken Aristotle a good five minutes to get from the cottage and up the embank-

ment to the railway line, but Bella positively

flew there in no time at all—to see a

terrifying sight.

On the railway track, a white cat was walking, sniffing curiously at the steel lines on either side of him, unaware that behind him an old steam train was coming into view, puffing and clanking and now, at the sight of the cat, whistling like mad.

Like a lot of white cats, Aristotle was a bit deaf, and he didn't take notice of the noise until the engine was nearly upon him, but then he heard Bella's voice.

"Lie down, Aristotle!" she screeched. "Lie down flat and don't move a whisker!"

Never did Aristotle forget the terrible

noise as the puffing whistling engine and its clanking rattling coaches passed right over him, only inches above, it seemed, as he lay between the rails.

(Never, what's more, did he ever go on the railway track again.)

As the noise died away, he opened his eyes, which, in his terror, he had kept shut tight, to see Bella Donna leaning on her broomstick by the edge of the track, and he ran to her and began to rub himself against her legs.

"Well, my boy," she said to him, "that was a near thing, wasn't it? Good thing you stayed still like I told you. You better watch out, Aristotle. Only four lives to go now." And she gave him a long look with her beady eyes.

At the lower end of Bella Donna's wood, there was a farm, to which Bella went to buy milk and eggs. Behind the farmhouse was a yard, and in the middle of the yard there stood a big wooden doghouse. Now that Aristotle was nearly full grown, he often walked down to the farm behind Bella, his white tail waving.

The first time he went there, she stopped at the yard gate and pointed to the doghouse.

"Don't go near that," she said to him, "or you'll be sorry. You wait here while I go and see the farmer's wife."

On the next few visits, Aristotle did indeed sit by the gate, staring at the dark opening in the doghouse until, one day, he thought he'd like to have a look inside it, and he set off across the yard.

As he got near, he smelled a strange smell coming from it, a smell that he'd never come across before and didn't much like, and then, when he was very close, he heard a noise. It was the noise of someone snoring.

Curious, as all cats are, Aristotle poked his head around the edge of the doghouse door and peered into the blackness of the interior. There, fast asleep, lying on its stomach, its great head upon its paws, lay a very large animal—the cause of the smell and the snores

It so happened that Aristotle had never before in his life seen a dog and did not know that most dogs don't much like cats. But the smell of this animal was now so strong in his nose and its snoring so loud in his ears that he thought he'd leave it in peace, especially as each snore drew back the creature's lips to show a battery of sharp-looking teeth.

Just as well, for this was not only a large dog but a very fierce dog, which the farmer kept to guard his farmyard. Around its thick neck was a heavy studded leather collar, and attached to this collar at one end and to a ringbolt in the doghouse at the other, was a length of heavy chain.

Little did Aristotle dream that this chain would soon save him from losing the last four of his lives in one fell swoop.

On the next couple of visits to the farm with Bella, Aristotle contented himself with just sitting and staring at the smell-filled, snore-loud doghouse. But then, one day, he decided that while Bella was buying her eggs and milk, he must just have another peep at the strange animal.

As before, he peered into the darkness within. As before, he saw the great sleeping shape. But then something very unfortunate happened. Maybe it was the dust from the dog's straw bedding, maybe it had to do with the smell of the creature, but suddenly Aristotle sneezed.

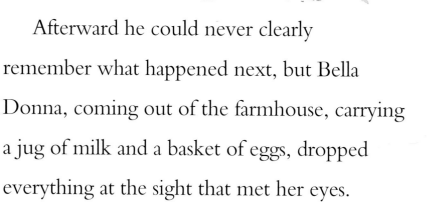

Afterward he could never clearly remember what happened next, but Bella Donna, coming out of the farmhouse, carrying a jug of milk and a basket of eggs, dropped everything at the sight that met her eyes.

With a volley of bloodcurdling growls, the big dog came hurtling out of its house, inches behind a wildly fleeing white cat, which it overtook and grabbed in its huge jaws.

But the dog's rush took it to the end of
its length of chain. Suddenly brought up
short, its head was jerked back, forcing its
jaws open, and out of them fell a
bewildered befuddled bedraggled Aristotle.

Back in the cottage, once Bella Donna had cleaned him up and satisfied herself that there were no bones broken, she addressed him in stern fashion.

"Well, my boy," she said, "you should have listened to me, shouldn't you? That was a close shave. You better watch your step, Aristotle. Only three lives to go."

She held him up before her face and looked into his pale eyes. Gazing back into her dark twinkling ones, Aristotle forgot his fright and snuggled thankfully against his friend.

Aristotle never went into the farmyard now. He would walk part of the way with Bella when she went to buy milk and eggs, but at the edge of the wood he'd stop and wait until she came back again.

Sometimes he would hear the barking of that awful monster that lived in the doghouse but he had no wish ever to see it again.

Then one day, months later, he did.

Bella was crossing the yard on her way to the farmhouse when she saw the farmer go to the doghouse and unclip the chain from the dog's collar. It then lumbered toward her, not in a threatening way, but with flattened ears, a wagging tail, and a sort of silly grin on its great face.

"Funny thing," the farmer said to her. "Old Gripper, why he's a devil with most people—bite 'em as soon as look at 'em, he will—but he seems to like you."

"I expect," said Bella, "that that's because he knows I'm not scared of him." And she put out a hand to the dog, and he slobbered over it.

"I'm letting him have a little run around this morning," the farmer said. "There's some boys been scrumping apples out of my orchard. Old Gripper'll soon chase them off."

For a while the dog sniffed about among the apple trees and then, making the most of the unaccustomed freedom,

vent toward the wood, his mind on rabbits.

But it was not a rabbit that saw him coming. It was a white cat.

At sight of the dog, Aristotle forgot all about waiting for Bella and took to his heels. Made silly by fright, he did not run back to the cottage but simply set off through the trees as fast as he could, without thinking where he was going. Seeing the railway embankment on one side and

not wishing to go there again, he turned in the opposite direction, heading, though he did not know it, straight for the road that ran along the other side of the wood.

Another thing he did not know was that he was being followed.

White is not the best color for an animal that wants to conceal itself among the greens and browns of woodland, and it was a flash of white that caught Gripper's eye as he left the orchard. Breaking into a lumbering run, he

came to the spot where he had sighted the cat.
It was nowhere to be seen, but the dog put
down his nose and began to follow the scent.

Someone else was following *him*.

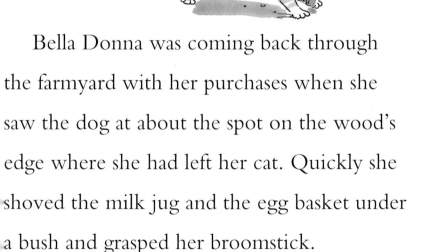

Bella Donna was coming back through
the farmyard with her purchases when she
saw the dog at about the spot on the wood's
edge where she had left her cat. Quickly she
shoved the milk jug and the egg basket under
a bush and grasped her broomstick.

Aristotle meanwhile had reached the twisty road that ran beside the wood. Thinking that he had outpaced the awful monster and so feeling less scared, he stopped to get his breath. But then he looked up the road to see another monster coming—a large delivery truck.

As he turned to get away from the nasty noisy thing, he came face to face with Gripper, who had been running silently on his trail and now dashed at him, open-mouthed.

"Never seen anything like it in my life before," the truck driver told his wife later. "There's this white cat, runs clean under my truck, between the wheels and out the other side, and then there's this big dog, been chasin the cat, and he tries to follow, and I bangs on my brakes, and then suddenly there's this old woman, appears from nowhere, she does, and she's carrying what looks like a broomstick,

and she gives the dog a great
whack with it, and he lets out a howl and runs
back into the wood, and I gets out and there's
no sign of any of 'em—cat, dog, old woman,
all disappeared."

"She had a broomstick, you say?" asked the truck driver's wife.

"Yes."

"Go on with you! Next thing, you'll be telling me she was all dressed in black, with tall black hat on her head!"

"She was."

Once Aristotle had gotten over his double fright of being chased by one monster and almost squashed by another, he managed somehow to make his way home to the cottage, to find Bella Donna at the kitchen fire, stirring something in

the cauldron. On the table stood a jug of
milk and a basket of eggs. In the corner
stood her broomstick.

He ran to her and began to rub himself
madly against her black-stockinged legs,
purring like a steam engine.

"Well, my boy," said Bella Donna, "that was a narrow squeak. I think we have to count that as two lives. Dog or truck— either would have killed you, Aristotle. So really, out of your nine lives, you've used up eight now. Your ninth life is going to have to last you a long, long time."

She picked up her white cat and stroked him thoughtfully.

"And I'll tell you something, Aristotle," she said to him. "I shouldn't be at all surprised now if it did."

When Bella Donna next went down to the farm, leaving Aristotle behind, of course, she went straight to the doghouse in the yard.

Gripper came out with a rush, only to pull himself to a halt—before the chain did—once he saw who it was. Bella tickled him behind his ears, and he wagged his tail madly.

"I've come to say I'm sorry," Bella told him. "I shouldn't have whacked you with my broomstick. Mind you, if I hadn't, you'd have run under the truck. But I must have hurt your feelings as well as your bottom. Will you forgive me?"

n reply, the big dog grinned at her and

icked her hand.

Now not just the months but the years

passed, and Aristotle grew into a fine cat

and a sensible cat, what's more. He didn't

get into any scrapes and, as Bella had

foreseen, he kept healthy and stayed safe,

happy in his long ninth life.

Dogs, however, have only one life, and

down at the farm Gripper had grown very

old. No longer did he rush out of his

house at the approach of strangers. No

longer did he try to bite anyone and

everyone. Mostly he lay in the yard at the end of his chain, thinking of days gone by.

One warm night he lay there, still, in the light of a full moon, and had the strangest of dreams.

In this dream he heard a swishing noise in the sky above and, raising his heavy head, looked up to see a dark shape flying across the face of the moon. It seemed to be riding on something, this dark shape did, and to have on its head a tall black hat. Sitting perched on its shoulder was a white shape, a shape that reminded Old

Gripper of something that had happened years ago. He gave one last great growl before his head dropped upon his paws, never to be raised again.

Strangely, when Bella next went down to the farm, Aristotle followed her as of old, white tail waving. He followed her right into the yard and right past the dark mouth of the doghouse. Stretched out from its door, the long chain lay on

the ground and at the end of it was the
heavy studded dog collar, unbuckled.

I expect you're wondering if Aristotle is still
enjoying his ninth life. Well, he is, I can
tell you, because he's now not only a grown-
up cat but he's a proper witch's cat too,
helping the good witch Bella Donna with her
work. Some of the strange mixtures that Bella
heats in her cauldron each day are food for her
and for her cat. But many are magic potions

or curing ailments, such as headaches or toothaches or tummyaches.

At night Bella climbs on her broomstick and flies off—Aristotle knows this because he goes with her—carrying these medicines to the homes of sick children, where she gives a spoonful of this or that to the child as it sleeps. Afterward she always makes sure that she and her cat are home by midnight.

Aristotle's quite an old fellow now, of course, and Bella Donna is an old old woman. Her gray hair is as white as the fur of her cat.

But they're still living happily together
in the old thatched cottage in the wood.
Bella Donna and Aristotle still have
a lot of time to enjoy each
other's company.